P9-CST-846

SOMETIMES IT'S HARD TO BE NICE

MAGGIE C. RUDD   illustrated by **KELLY O'NEILL**

Albert Whitman & Company • Chicago, Illinois

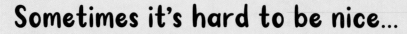

Sometimes it's hard to be nice...

Like when your cousin comes over and takes the ONLY toy you want to play with, and your mom says you have to share.

So you wait and wait and WAIT until he is finished.
And when you get it back, one of the wheels is broken.

Sometimes being nice is really hard.

Sometimes it's hard to be nice...

Like when you have to go to your sister's dance recital and you just want to play outside instead.

But you go anyway because she's your sister,
and you sit through it even though it's the WORST.
And then she kisses you for being there!

Ugh!

Sometimes it's hard to be nice...

Like when you are really hungry and your grandma gives you tuna noodle casserole, and you HATE tuna noodle casserole, and you really, really, REALLY don't want to eat the tuna noodle casserole.

But you don't want to hurt Grandma's feelings.

So you force down a few bites and thank her for dinner.

Even though you don't feel very thankful.

Sometimes being nice takes practice...

Like when your baby brother rips all the
pages out of your books. For no reason.

And you scream and stomp and call him
THE MEANEST BROTHER IN THE WHOLE ENTIRE WORLD!

But then you clean up the mess. Because you know he is just a little kid. And sometimes little kids haven't learned how to be nice yet.

Sometimes being nice takes practice...

Like when you go to visit your great-grandpa
who just moved into the nursing home.
And you're so excited to see him.

But when you get there, it smells funny, and you feel nervous. And your dad tells you to come say hello to your great-grandpa, but you are scared so you don't.

But next time you will.
Next time.

Sometimes being nice takes practice...

Like when you have been waiting in line for the big slide, and a kid jumps in front of you because he didn't see you standing there.

And your mom says that the polite thing to do is to let him go first.

But it's your turn so you go anyway.
Somehow it isn't as fun.
Next time you'll let him go first.

Sometimes being nice feels good...

Like when your baby brother wants to learn how to play your favorite game but he is too small.

So you let him sit with you while you play so he can watch.

And he claps for you the whole time.

Sometimes being nice feels good...

Like when you and the boy next door play really hard all day with your new Galactic Star Crusher action figures, and you make a big mess.

And later you pick up all the toys even though
nobody asked you to.
And your dad scoops you up and squeezes
you tight and says he is proud of you.
And that is better than any action figure.

Sometimes being nice feels good...

Like when you are late for soccer practice and your mom can't find her keys, so you help her look for them.

And after searching everywhere, you finally find them in the doorknob!

And your mom says she doesn't know what she would do without you!

And you're so happy that you helped.

Sometimes being nice takes courage...

Like when there's a kid at school that everyone picks on. And one day you see the kid alone playing with the Galactic Star Crusher action figure that you've been wanting.

So you go up to him and ask him if he wants to play.

Even though you know you might
get picked on too because of it.

Sometimes being nice takes courage...

Like when the bigger kids ask you if you are friends with *that* kid.

And it turns out that *that* kid likes the same stuff you like. He even shared his cookies with you at lunch.

So you swallow, and you say, "Yes," because you ARE friends with that kid.

Sometimes being nice takes courage...

Like when your new friend is in trouble and you stand up for him even though you are really scared. Because he is your friend.

And he sits with you while you wait in the principal's office, and you know you aren't alone.

Sometimes being nice is hard.
And it can even be a little scary...

but it's worth it.

For Alex—MR
For Mom and Dad—KO

Library of Congress Cataloging-in-Publication data is on file with the publisher.

Text copyright © 2021 by Maggie C. Rudd
Illustrations copyright © 2021 by Albert Whitman & Company
Illustrations by Kelly O'Neill
First published in the United States of America in 2021 by Albert Whitman & Company
ISBN 978-0-8075-7573-4 (hardcover)
ISBN 978-0-8075-7579-6 (ebook)
Printed in China
10 9 8 7 6 5 4 3 2 1 WKT 24 23 22 21 20

Design by Aphelandra

For more information about Albert Whitman & Company,
visit our website at www.albertwhitman.com.